# TALES FROM CHINA

# *OUTLAWS* of the *MARSH*

Vol.
03

# OUTLAWS of the MARSH

**Vol. 03**

## Lost In Exile

### Created by WEI DONG CHEN

*Wei Dong Chen is a highly acclaimed artist and an influential leader
in the "New Chinese Cartoon" trend. He is the founder of Creator World,
the largest comics studio in China. His spirited and energetic work has attracted
many students to his tutelage. He has published more than 300 cartoons in
several countries and gained both recognition and admirers across Asia, Europe,
and the USA. Mr. Chen's work is serialized in several publications,
and he continues to explore new dimensions of the graphic medium.*

### Illustrated by XIAO LONG LIANG

*Xiao Long Liang is considered one of Wei Dong Chen's greatest students.
One of the most highly regarded cartoonists in China today, Xiao Long's
fantastic technique and expression of Chinese culture have won him
the acclaim of cartoon lovers throughout China.*

**Original Story**
**"The Water Margin"** by Shi, Nai An

**Editing & Designing**
Mybloomy, Jonathan Evans, KH Lee, YK Kim,
HJ Lee, JS Kim, Lampin, Qing Shao, Xiao Nan Li, Ke Hu

DEC − − 2015

## CHONG LIN

Chong Lin is a former Marshal of the Imperial Guard. When the villainous son of Grand Marshal Qiu Gao took a liking to Chong Lin's wife, the latter was framed for a crime and sentenced to exile. Along the way, the two men charged with escorting him into exile tried to kill him, but ZhiShen Lu appeared and saved Chong Lin's life. Now, Chong Lin will reach his destination, but that doesn't mean he's out of danger. And if he's not careful, he will soon find himself on the run for actual crimes, and not just false charges.

## JIN CHAI

Master Jin Chai is a descendant of Emperor ShiZhong of the Zhou Dynasty. Now that his family is no longer in control of the nation, Jin Chai spends his time helping those who need it in his home city of CanZhou. This includes the occasional outlaw, whom Jin Chai sends to the mysterious LiangShan Marsh.

## THE WARDEN OF CANGZHOU PRISON

A local government official responsible for the prison in CangZhou, the warden is a man whose corruption is limitless. He routinely takes bribes from prisoners for better treatment, yet is not opposed to killing a prisoner for the right price. So when Chong Lin comes to CangZhou prison, the warden must decide who to favor: those who want his newest prisoner treated well, or those who want him dead.

## XIAOER LI

XiaoEr Li is a tavern owner in CangZhou. Years before, he was living as a waiter in DongJing when he was accused of a crime. Chong Lin, still a marshal of the Imperial Guard at the time, spoke well of XiaoEr Li, and the courts showed him mercy. Years later, the two men meet again, and XiaoEr Li offers to repay his life debt to Chong Lin by being his eyes and ears while he's in exile.

# Characters

## GUI ZHU

Gui Zhu is a bandit of LiangShan who runs a tavern at the edge of the marsh to keep one eye on those who pass near the bandits' hidden fortress. Gui Zhu's suspicions are raised when Chong Lin comes into his tavern and asks where he can hire a boat, but soon the two men are talking, and Gui Zhu decides Chong Lin would be a valuable addition to their ranks.

## LUN WANG

With the help of Jin Chai, Lun Wang established WanZi Fortress at LiangShan Marsh as a haven for those who had been wronged by a corrupt government. When Chong Lin arrives, Lun Wang feels threatened by the accomplished marshal. But soon Lun Wang sees the advantage of Chong Lin joining them, so he accepts him as the fourth bandit captain of LiangShan.

## ZHI YANG

Zhi Yang is an officer of the Song Dynasty who is tasked with transporting a large shipment of minerals. When a sudden storm causes Zhi Yang to lose the entire shipment, he reluctantly decides to return to the capital of DongJing to report his failure. Along the way he passes near LiangShan Marsh, where Chong Lin attacks him in order to fulfill a pledge to Lun Wang. But Chong Lin has underestimated his opponent, and Zhi Yang will not make an easy target.

# Chapter 1

# *Chong Lin in Exile*

## Summary

Chong Lin has come to CangZhou to serve out a sentence of exile for a crime he did not commit. Upon his arrival, he met a local dignitary named Master Jin Chai, a known benefactor who aids those in need. Jin Chai gives Chong Lin a letter to deliver to the warden of the CangZhou prison, where Chong Lin will be incarcerated. The letter asks for Chong Lin to be treated well, and the warden obliges. Chong Lin is sent to a remote temple and given the easy job of keeping it clean.

But trouble has followed Chong Lin to CangZhou. Qian Lu, Chong Lin's former friend and the man who framed him in the first place, arrives in the city and asks the warden to kill Chong Lin. The warden accepts a large bribe and tries to have Chong Lin taken care of. But luck is on Chong Lin's side, and he narrowly escapes death. In the aftermath, though, Chong Lin will commit acts he never thought possible, and soon he's in hiding for crimes worse than the false ones that brought him here.

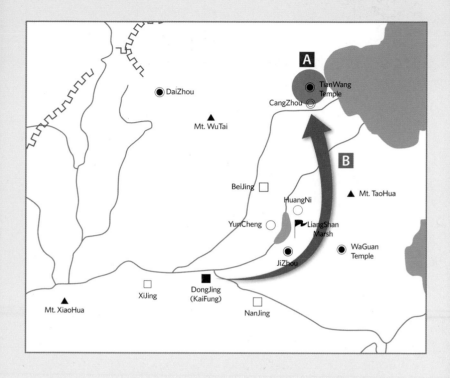

**A** Chong Lin, serving his sentence in exile, is appointed caretaker of TianWang Temple.

**B** Qian Lu, carrying orders from Grand Marshal Qiu Gao, arrives in CangZhou and asks the warden to kill Chong Lin.

Chong Lin continued his journey into exile, accompanied by the two men who had earlier tried to kill him. Not long after parting ways with ZhiShen Lu, who swore to kill the two escorts if they harmed their captive, Chong Lin met the esteemed Jin Chai, a known benefactor.

Jin Chai lived up to his reputation, and wrote a letter asking the warden of CangZhou prison to treat Chong Lin with dignity and respect, two things commonly denied prisoners.

The three men wound their way through the streets of CangZhou toward the local prison.

Upon their arrival, Chong Lin was handed over to the local authorities for incarceration.

WELL, THIS IS IT. WHAT WILL YOU DO NOW?

WHAT ELSE? WE'LL GO BACK TO DONGJING.

*HUH.* I WONDER WHAT THEY'LL SAY.

15

ALL RIGHT, MAGGOTS! ON YOUR FEET!

THAT MUST BE THE JAILER!

GOOD. BELIEVE ME, I DON'T WANT TO SEE ANYONE ELSE'S EYE PLUCKED OUT BECAUSE HE COULDN'T SCROUNGE UP A FEW COINS.

KREEK

WHERE'S OUR NEW GUEST?

RIGHT HERE.

21

23

Chong Lin did as he was instructed. He swept the floors of the temple and burned incense every day. Before he knew it, six whole weeks had passed.

And the warden and jailer were as good as their word. They kept an eye out for Chong Lin, and made sure no harm came to him while he was under their watch.

BRR
IT'S ALREADY WINTER...

Some time later, Chong Lin was out for a stroll when he ran into someone from his past.

WAIT. DO I KNOW YOU?

WAIT. I *DO* KNOW YOU! YOU ARE MARSHAL CHONG LIN FROM DONGJING, AREN'T YOU?

I AM, WHY DO YOU--HANG ON. XIAOER LI, IS THAT YOU? WHAT ARE YOU DOING HERE?

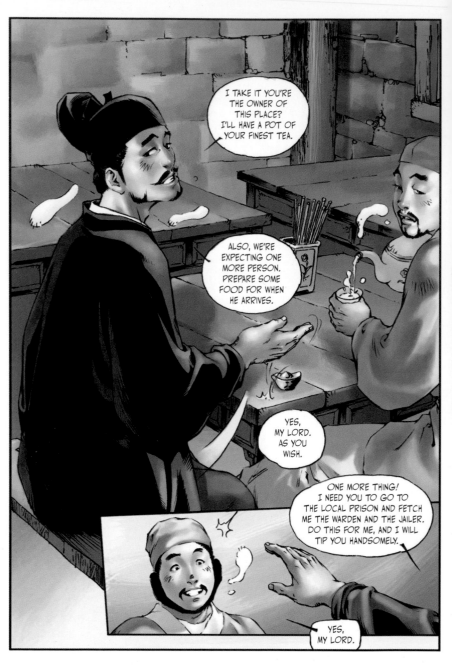

An hour later, XiaoEr Li returned with the warden and the jailer.

GUH! IT'S TOO DAMN COLD TO BE OUT!

WHO THE HELL SUMMONED US?

I'M ASSUMING IT'S THIS MAN. MAY I ASK YOUR NAME?

MY NAME IS NOT IMPORTANT. PLEASE, SIT DOWN. POUR YOURSELF A DRINK.

MY FRIEND, WE INTEND TO DISCUSS PRIVATE MATTERS. I'LL ASK YOU TO LEAVE US ALONE NOW.

OF COURSE.

35

WHERE ARE YOU? EVERY PIG LEAVES A TRAIL OF FILTH BEHIND.

Chong Lin tucked a dagger into his clothes and scoured the city for Qian Lu, but days later he still hadn't found a single trace of him.

A short time later, the prison warden put Chong Lin in charge of maintaining a supply depot for the winter.

The warden told Chong Lin that he was being promoted to a better job, but Chong Lin couldn't help noticing how the new job took him to the farthest and most remote part of CangZhou.

KREEK

FWOOOSH

PACK UP, OLD MAN. THE WARDEN'S ORDERED YOU AND CHONG LIN TO SWITCH JOBS.

BUT WHY DON'T YOU GIVE HIM THE GRAND TOUR FIRST?

YES, MY LORD.

41

THAT'S MY CANTEEN. IF YOU NEED A DRINK, THERE'S A TAVERN DOWN THE ROAD.

THANK YOU.

GOOD LUCK.

SAFE TRAVELS.

HYOOOM

BRR! IT'S GOING TO BE A LONG WINTER IF I HAVE TO LIVE HERE.

KRACK

SZZZ

FWUMP

GREAT. NOW I HAVE SOMETHING TO REPAIR WHEN IT STOPS SNOWING.

HWOOOH

GUH, THIS COLD SEEPS INTO THE BONES. THINK I'LL GRAB A DRINK TO WARM UP A BIT.

KLACK

FWAP

GOOD EVENING, SIR. WHERE MIGHT YOU BE FROM?

I DON'T SUPPOSE YOU RECOGNIZE THIS CANTEEN?

SURE I DO! IT BELONGS TO THE OLD MAN WHO MAINTAINS THE SUPPLY DEPOT.

USED TO. NOW I'M THE ONE WHO LIVES IN THE SHACK.

WELL, WELCOME! HOW ABOUT A DRINK TO FIGHT THIS CHILL?

THANK YOU. I'D ALSO ASK YOU TO FILL MY CANTEEN AND WRAP UP SOME BEEF.

YOU GOT IT.

SEE YOU AROUND.

STAY WARM AND DRY.

FWAP

AT LEAST THE BEDDING STAYED DRY.

BUT NOW I'VE GOT NO PLACE TO SLEEP. GUESS I HAVEN'T SPENT MY LAST NIGHT SLEEPING IN A TEMPLE AFTER ALL.

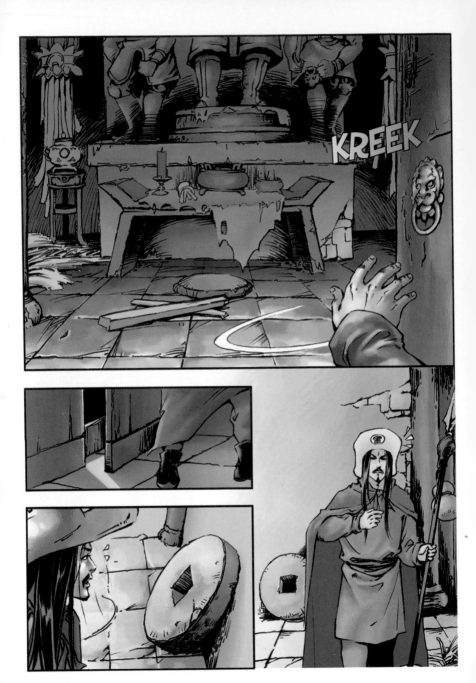

THMP THMP

...AND YOU'RE SURE EVERYTHING WILL GO AS PLANNED?

WAIT A MINUTE. I KNOW THOSE VOICES...

OF COURSE! BY THIS TIME TOMORROW, CHONG LIN WILL BE A MEMORY.

HWOOOAH

HE'D BETTER BE. ONLY WHEN HE'S DEAD WILL YANEI GAO BE SATISFIED.

VERY WELL. IF THIS WORKS, YOU WILL BE REWARDED BY QIU GAO. I PROMISE.

RELAX. THE KING OF HELL WOULD BE SCORCHED BY THESE FLAMES.

AT LAST! I HAVEN'T SLEPT IN MONTHS. BUT WITH CHONG LIN DEAD, I'LL GET A GOOD NIGHT'S SLEEP.

79

THIS ISN'T OVER, YOU BASTARD! I'M COMING BACK, AND I'M BRINGING MY FRIENDS!

BRING AS MANY AS WISH TO DIE!

COME ON!

HA HA HA!

85

# Chapter 2

# The Fogs of LiangShan

## Summary

Chong Lin has taken shelter with Master Jin Chai, but he knows the authorities will not stop hunting him, so he decides to leave and not endanger the man who's been so kind to him. Jin Chai gives Chong Lin letters of recommendation and sneaks him out of CangZhou, setting him on a course for the mysterious WanZi Fortress at LiangShan Marsh. When he comes to a tavern on the edge of the marsh, Chong Lin meets Gui Zhu, one of the leaders of WanZi, who hails a boat to take them through LiangShan.

Chong Lin meets with the other three bandit leaders: Lun Wang, Qian Du, and Wang Sun. All embrace Chong Lin save for Lun Wang, who sees him as a threat and demands that a pledge be fulfilled first. Chong Lin is given three days to find and kill a man, or else he will not be permitted to live in LiangShan. Chong Lin reluctantly accepts the challenge, but when he encounters a resilient adversary named Zhi Yang, there is an unlikely shift in the balance of power in LiangShan.

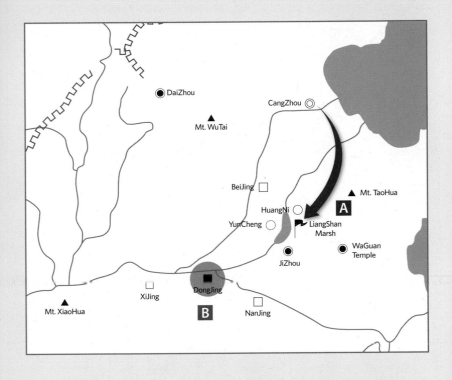

**A** Jin Chai escorts the fugitive Chong Lin out of CangZhou and sends him toward LiangShan Marsh.

**B** Zhi Yang, a dynasty official who lost a shipment of precious cargo, returns to DongJing to admit his fault and beg for mercy.

ALL RIGHT, PAY ATTENTION. THIS HERE IS CHONG LIN.

Chong Lin was well aware that a manhunt was underway. With each passing day, he felt more uneasy about hiding in Jin Chai's manor.

MASTER JIN CHAI, YOU KNOW THE AUTHORITIES WON'T STOP LOOKING FOR ME.

HE'S WANTED FOR THE MURDER OF THREE PUBLIC OFFICIALS.

IT'S ONLY A MATTER OF TIME BEFORE THEY SEARCH THIS PLACE. I NEED TO LEAVE.

YES, I KNOW.

THE ONE WHO CATCHES HIM WILL RECEIVE 3,000 GOLD COINS.

ANYONE CAUGHT HARBORING HIM WILL LOSE HIS HEAD.

161

The five men celebrated long into the night, and Zhi Yang departed the next morning.

SAFE JOURNEY, ZHI YANG. BEST OF LUCK.

AND TO YOU. I WILL NEVER FORGET THE LIANGSHAN BANDITS.

From that moment on, Lin Chong was considered one of the leaders of LiangShan Marsh.

Meanwhile, Zhi Yang had returned to DongJing, hoping to beg and bribe his way out of trouble.

WELCOME, MY LORD. WILL YOU NEED A PLACE TO STAY?

YES. ONE WITH A VIEW.

ANYTHING ELSE THEN?

PLINK

I'LL TAKE WHATEVER'S HOT. ALL OF IT!

YES, SIR!

A few days later, Zhi Yang met with a man he hired to broker his reinstatement as a public official.

HERE. A SMALL TOKEN OF MY APPRECIATION FOR YOUR EFFORTS.

# *Chong Lin in Exile*

Chong Lin is the tragic hero in the early chapters of *Outlaws of the Marsh*, an honorable man who served his emperor with distinction and loved his wife with all his heart. Fidelity to nation and family are two cherished principles in any culture at any time, and Chong Lin believes that adhering to those principles makes him a good man. But when corruption and villainy conspire to frame Chong Lin for a crime and sentence him to exile, he learns that when principle, purpose, and social order have been stripped away, he is nothing like the man he thought he was.

From the beginning, there were suggestions of a violent nature lurking beneath Chong Lin's calm demeanor: when YaNei Gao first made unwanted advances on his wife, Chong Lin struggled to suppress the impulse to kill him, since such an act against the son of a royal official would result in a death sentence. But even once he'd overcome the impulse, he tormented himself with thoughts of how helpless he was in the face of social norms and the law itself. When YaNei Gao conspired with Qian Lu to have him exiled, Chong Lin learned that the law did not deliver justice. But Chong Lin will realize that his idea of justice can be just as vicious as anything done to him by YaNei Gao.

Once he is sentenced to exile, Chong Lin is expelled from the social order he relied on so heavily. As a result, there is no one to defend his life and no way to seek retribution if he is further wronged. If he is to survive, Chong Lin must become a society unto himself and act as guardian, judge, and jury, so that he alone defines what justice is. When Qian Lu betrays Chong Lin a second time, and tries to kill him by setting fire to the military supply depot, Chong Lin sentences his old friend and his two companions to death and carries out the sentence with the swift brutality of a natural born killer. Chong Lin is startled by the realization that he can do something so violent, so ruthless, so against his nature. But then he must consider that by doing what he's done, his nature wasn't all that good to begin with.

Chong Lin's story asks the reader to consider the role of society in shaping an individual's identity and what defines goodness. If a man is capable of violence, but never commits a violent act because it is against the laws of society, should he be considered a violent person? If a person is capable of breaking the law but doesn't, is he still an outlaw? How much are we defined by actions that are kept in check by laws, and how does that impact our sense of who we are? For Chong Lin, the answer is obvious, because his entire sense of self is destroyed when society fails him: Of all the things he lost in exile, the most important thing he lost was himself.

ZHI YANG